TRIBADISM 1

THE ART OF LESBIAN LOVE

VICTORIA RUSH

VOLUME 44

JADE'S EROTIC ADVENTURES - BOOK 44

COPYRIGHT

For the uninhibited...

WANT TO AMP UP YOUR SEX LIFE?

Sign up for my newsletter to receive more free books and other steamy stuff. Discover a hundred different ways to wet your whistle!

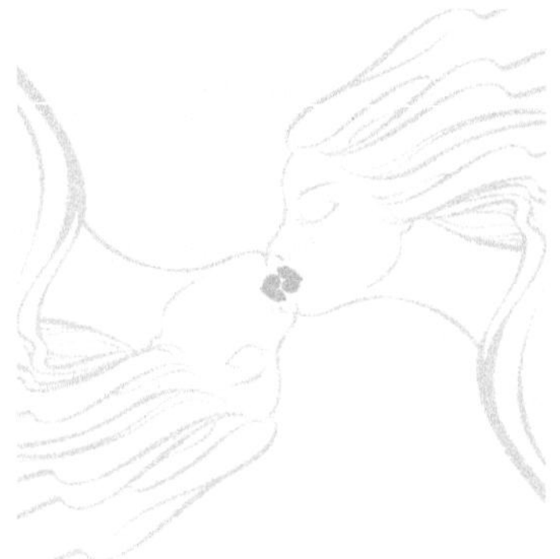

Victoria Rush Erotica

1

———

When I received a message from my intimacy coach announcing a new all-girls workshop, my heart skipped a beat. But when I discovered it would be focused entirely on learning new tribbing techniques, a *different* part of my anatomy began throbbing. The idea of a group of naked women practicing new scissoring positions in full view of each other was impossible to resist. I booked a flight to New York for the next available session and was barely able to sit still the entire trip.

When I arrived at Laila's Upper West Side apartment on the scheduled day, she greeted me at the door with a soft kiss. Her co-op was decorated with the same tasteful Georgia O'Keefe and Japanese shunga art that I remembered, but instead of the reclining lounge chairs from her last session, this time her living room was set up with a series of large yoga mats arrayed in a circle around a single, vinyl-covered futon.

Some of the other workshop attendees had already arrived, and we introduced ourselves as we sampled hors d'oeuvres laid out on the buffet table, while soft instrumental music played in the background. I recognized a few of the women from the previous session where we'd learned how to squirt at her Fountain of Venus workshop. The pretty young redhead, Piper, had returned, along with the sexy blonde, Hailey, and the hot African-American lesbian, Trinity.

But the rest of the women looked unfamiliar and my pussy grew increasingly moist as I casually flitted around the room, sampling the buffet fare. Most of the girls had already changed into terrycloth robes laid out on hooks lining the entrance hall, and as we chatted amongst ourselves, Laila circulated amongst us making small talk, trying to ease the nervous tension in the room. With her long, silver-blonde hair, bright blue eyes, and taut, Madonna-like figure, I couldn't help stealing glances at her sexy body whenever her back was turned.

When the last attendee arrived and everybody had changed into their robes, Laila asked us to take a seat on one of the yoga mats and make ourselves comfortable. But with only half as many mats as workshop participants, each of us had to sit knee-to-knee beside one another in pairs. Whether this was by design or accident, I couldn't be sure, but as my exposed thigh brushed up against the young redhead's sitting next to me, I felt goosebumps beginning to spread over my body.

"Thank you all for coming," Laila said, sitting cross-legged on the futon while peering at each of the women arranged around the circle. "I recognize a few familiar faces from our last workshop. I hope you've been enjoying some of the new techniques we learned together."

"*Um-hmm,*" Hailey hummed, with a sly smile on her face. "It's a good thing these mats are made out of *rubber,*" she said, rubbing her fingers softly across the surface of her yoga cushion. "Because ever since you taught me how to ejaculate, I seem to make a mess out of every place I have sex!"

"Well, I'm hoping that isn't always a *bad* thing," Laila smiled while clasping her hands over her lap as I tried to steal glances under her partially open robe.

"Absolutely!" Hailey said, leaning back on her outstretched arms to reveal the dark cleft between her parted knees.

"Our focus for this workshop is going to be a little *different*," Laila said. "Although if it involves a little extra waterworks, that should only add to the excitement. In this session, we're going to learn about the many different ways women can connect their bodies together. How many of you have touched another woman in this way?"

Many of the women around the circle raised their hands, while a few looked at Laila with puzzled expressions.

"Does kissing girls during middle-school sleepovers count?" a pretty brunette sitting on the opposite side of the circle asked.

"Yes, but I was thinking of touching in more intimate places..."

"With what *parts* of our bodies exactly?" another woman asked. "I went down on my roommate once after a drunken binge during college–"

"Those are all lovely ways to connect with your partner," Laila nodded. "But since the subject of this workshop is *trib-adism*, I meant in a very specific way."

"You mean *scissoring*?" Piper said, bumping her knee excitedly against mine.

"That's another word for it, yes," Laila said. "Although technically, tribbing means to *rub*, so tribadism involves rubbing *any* two body parts together, though most of the time it involves stimulating the vulvas in one form or another. So, with that slightly more limited definition, how many of you have indulged with members of your same sex that way?"

A smaller number of women raised their hands and Laila nodded.

"And for those of you who've practiced the specific art of scissoring, how many different *positions* have you tried or discovered?"

"Five or six?" a pink-haired girl said, pinching her eyebrows together.

"Maybe ten or twelve," an attractive middle-aged woman suggested.

"How many different ways can two women *connect* that way?" the African-American girl, Trinity, said. "I mean, there's only so many ways we can twist our bodies and rub our pussies together."

"You might be surprised," Laila said. "Did you know there are over a hundred different ways two women can stimulate themselves without using their hands or lips? Even more if you add other partners into the mix."

"Will we be learning all of these positions at this work-shop?" Piper asked, flapping her legs together in growing excitement.

"We probably won't have time to practice *all* of them here," Laila smiled. "But since this is a three-day workshop, we should be able to cover a lot of ground, in a manner of speaking."

"Including with multiple partners?" Hailey asked, peering around the circle with a raised eyebrow.

"On our last day, yes," Laila nodded. "But let's not get ahead of ourselves. We're going to take it one step at a time, starting with the basics and building up our repertoire of increasingly advanced positions while we go. Are you ready to get started?"

"Damn straight," Hailey said, pulling open her robe to reveal her firm, cantaloupe-sized tits. "I'm already starting to get pretty worked up with all this talk of pussy rubbing."

"Well then," Laila smiled. "Would you like to be my first volunteer? It'll be easier to demonstrate the positions with an assistant–"

"You're twisting my arm," Hailey said, rising up on her knees expectantly.

"Or your *legs*, as the case may be," Laila chuckled, patting the futon beside her. "Why don't you come join me so we can demonstrate the first position together?"

"Okay," Hailey said, prancing over to the middle of the circle and hopping down on the futon beside Laila. "How would you like me to position myself this first time?"

"As I said, we're going to work into this slowly," Laila smiled. "Partly to help those who've never done this before to get used to the idea of rubbing their bodies against another woman, but also so we can build up to more exciting and interesting positions. For our first demonstration, I'd like you to lie down on the mattress face up, with your legs spread a couple of feet apart."

"Naked, or with my robe on?" Hailey grinned, lying down beside Laila and looking up at her innocently.

"Whichever you prefer," Laila said, raising up and kneeling between Hailey's legs while facing her stomach. "Of course, it will be easier for the other women to see how we're engaging if we're both unclothed."

"I was *hoping* you'd say that," Hailey said, pulling off her robe and throwing it onto the floor beside the futon.

"For this first position," Laila said as nervous laughter spread around the room, "I'm going to demonstrate the *missionary* position with one woman lying on top of the other while we press our hips together."

Laila took off her robe and placed it on the floor atop Hailey's, and as everyone around the room stared at her impeccably shaped ass, she placed her hands on the futon beside Hailey's chest then lowered herself onto her body with her legs positioned straight behind her. When her mound pressed against Hailey's, Hailey tried to tilt her hips upward and spread her knees further apart to create friction on her clit, but she frowned peering into Laila's face positioned a foot above hers.

"This doesn't seem like much fun," she said, squirming awkwardly under Laila's pressing body. "I can't even rub my *pussy* against yours in this position."

"It's not designed to," Laila grinned, pulling her body higher up over Hailey's hips while she ground her vulva into her prone partner's mound. "This position is designed more for the superior partner's enjoyment."

She tilted her head to the side, looking back in the direction of the women seated in the circle behind her.

"For those of you at the six o'clock position behind me, can you see how I'm rubbing my vulva on my partner's pubis?"

The women behind her lowered their heads and nodded excitedly.

"Yes," one of them said, squirming slowly on her mat.

"This position is useful if one of you wants to assume the dominant position while focusing primarily on your *own* pleasure," Laila smiled, rocking her pussy firmly against Hailey's pinned hips.

She placed her hands on Hailey's big melons, squeezing them tightly while pinching her nipples.

"But you're also in a perfect position to stimulate *other*

parts of your partner's body with this posture. And it's a great way to gaze into her eyes while you're pleasuring yourself and spreading your lubrication all over her stomach and mound."

"Mmm," Hailey purred, writhing her hips under Laila's gyrating ass. "I can feel you dripping on me already. This is *way* sexier than I imagined–"

"Plus," Laila said, lowering her face toward Hailey's. "You're also in a perfect position to *kiss* your partner while your rub your bodies together..."

Laila placed her lips on Hailey's and began kissing her passionately, moaning into her mouth. While everyone around the circle stared at the couple squirming in vicarious excitement, Laila began pressing her pubis harder against Hailey's as she flexed her buttock muscles in rhythmic contractions. From my perspective forty-five degrees behind the couple, I could see her wet slit sliding atop Hailey's glistening mound as her juices began to dribble out of her pussy and down between Hailey parted thighs.

"Oh my *God*..." Piper murmured beside me as her hand began moving softly under her robe while she watched the action. "That is *so* fucking hot!"

"Not bad for a seemingly boring position with one partner fucking the other in the traditional top-over-bottom position, is it?" Laila said, lifting herself off Hailey and sitting beside her on the futon in a cross-legged position.

"Hey!" Hailey said, peering up at Laila with a surprised expression. "I was just getting warmed up! Why did you stop so quickly?"

"This workshop is all about teaching you how to pleasure your *own* partners," Laila said, glancing over at the empty spot left on Hailey's mat. "There's a reason why I invited an even number of participants to the workshop. I'm guessing your seatmate would rather try this technique out for herself than just watch. If you guys feel comfortable, now's the time for everyone to pair up and try this position out for yourselves."

"Okay, but who decides who'll be on top?" Hailey said, returning to her position on her mat.

"That's up to the two of you," Laila smiled. "But don't fret about it too much. By the time we finish today, each of you will have multiple opportunities to position yourselves with different partners. I wouldn't worry too much about who goes where this first time. Just ease into it slowly while you savor the feeling of another woman's body caressing yours."

"I like the sound of that," Hailey said, lying down beside her partner and spreading her legs apart to reveal her glistening pussy. "I could use another shower after experimenting with the bidet in my hotel room last night. But I have a feeling *this* one's going to be even more exciting with a live person squirting on me..."

2

While the rest of the girls began to pull off their robes, Piper turned toward me looking like a deer caught in the headlights.

"How would you like to do this?" she said with a breaking voice. "Would you like to be the one on top or on the bottom?"

"Whichever you prefer," I smiled, becoming even more turned on by her apparent lack of experience in these matters.

"I suppose I should be on the bottom, with you being the more, um, *experienced* between us."

"That's the nicest way someone's told me that I'm old in a long time," I chuckled. "But I think I might enjoy it even more with *you* taking the lead. That way, you'll be able to learn what works best for you while I lie back and watch your pleasure."

I pulled off my robe and folded it on the floor beside me, then lay down on the double-wide mat, spreading my legs slowly apart. Piper glanced up and down my figure, lingering a little longer staring at my bald mound and glistening slit as a trickle of lubrication cascaded down between my crack.

"Wow," she said, darting her eyes back and forth over my exposed body. "You're stunning."

"You're very beautiful too," I said, peering up into her hazel eyes. "Take off your robe and let's see what we have to work with."

Piper pulled off her gown one arm at a time then placed it atop mine beside the mat. As she kneeled innocently before me, I ran my eyes up and down her slender, fair-skinned figure. Her skin had an alabaster, almost transparent tone, with tiny freckles on the top of her chest and upper cheeks where she'd had the most exposure to the sun. Her breasts were smaller than mine, but firm and upstanding with bright pink nipples, already hardening as her areolas puckered in obvious excitement.

Her pussy was shaved clean like mine, and as I peered between her splayed legs, I could see the bump of her clitoris protruding between her parted labia. I desperately wanted to jump on top of her and suck her button into my mouth and it took every ounce of my willpower to remain still awaiting her first move.

"Oh my God, Piper," I gushed. "You're absolutely luminous. Come lay that gorgeous body on top of me so I can feel your exquisite skin on mine."

I raised my knees a few inches above the floor and spread my legs wider apart inviting her to come closer, and as she stared at my dripping slit, she knelt in front of me, slowly lowering her upper body onto mine. When I felt her cool skin on mine, I moaned, throwing my arms around her back and pulling her closer, thrusting my tongue into her mouth.

"Mmm," I moaned, feeling her hipbones pressing against

mine. "Rub your pussy against my mound. I want to feel your juices dripping all over me.

"Your breasts feel so soft," she panted, tilting her hips toward mine while she began to grind her cunny into my hard pubic bone. "I've never been with a woman this way."

"You're in for a treat then," I smiled, biting her upper lip softly. "There's nothing quite like the feeling of another woman rubbing her naked body against your own."

"So you've done this *before*?" she said.

"Maybe a few times," I smiled.

"Is there a right way to do it?" Piper said, swiping her mound awkwardly across mine.

"I'm not sure there's ever a *right* way for two women to caress one another," I said. "Just do what feels natural and pleasurable. There's no rush."

Piper turned her head to look at some of the other couples around the circle who'd already begun to moan and grind their hips together while writhing their bodies in unison atop their mats.

"It looks like some of the other women have found a way to stimulate their pussies more effectively than me," she said. "With my legs extended directly behind me the way Laila demonstrated, I can only seem to touch my bone against yours."

Overhearing her comment, Laila shuffled up next to the two of us, placing her hands atop Piper's buttocks.

"You've got to tilt your hips forward a few degrees to bring your sensitive parts higher up on your partner's mound," she instructed, peering into my eyes. "You might need to separate your stomach from Jade's while you arch your back in the shape of a camel's. Remember, you're the one in charge here, and you can do whatever feels best for you."

Piper did as Laila instructed, then she gasped when her nub slid over my bald mound.

"Huh!" she grunted, flinging her eyes wide open.

"Does that feel better?" Laila said, smiling toward me.

"Yes," she panted, beginning to rock her hips rhythmically over my hips as she rolled her clit over my skin.

"Let your *partner* guide you as well," she said, pulling my hands up over the back of Piper's flexing ass. "Her caresses and feedback will add to the excitement of the experience. Try to use *every* part of your bodies to stimulate one another while you're in this position."

As Laila pulled away to focus on other areas of the circle, I peered up at her and nodded. I appreciated her helpful guidance, but even more so I envied her role as the master of ceremonies being able to watch everyone as they engaged with their partners in such intimate surroundings. It must have been a feast for her eyes to take in the sight of all the couples grinding their naked bodies together while she sat back and took it all in.

"Lift yourself up on your arms a bit so I can see your face and play with your breasts," I said to Piper. "Like the lady said, being in the missionary position doesn't have to mean we're restricted to rubbing only our *hips* together. This will also give you a better angle to rub your pussy against my mound."

"Ungh," Piper groaned, propping herself up a few inches, tilting her pussy toward the lower curvature of my pubis.

"Better?" I said, holding her flexing buttock muscles in my hands.

"*Better*," she panted, gazing into my eyes while a soft flush began to roll over her pale cheeks.

I moved my hands up to her tits and cupped them softly, pinching her nipples between my fingers as I rocked my hips in concert with hers. Although the contact point between our hips negated any direct contact on my clitoris while lying prone on the floor, the movement of her wet pussy over the tip of my mound was driving me insane with desire as I watched her pleasure continuing to mount.

"*Yes*, Piper," I panted. "Fuck my mound with your pretty pussy. I can feel your juices running down my slit while I watch you getting more turned on."

"Yes," she grunted, placing her hands over my breasts as she humped my hips. "Squeeze my nipples while I fuck you. This is so sexy, making love to your beautiful body."

"You're *enjoying* being on top then?" I smiled, pinching her nipples harder as she began to rock her hips more rapidly over my hard pubis.

"*Fuck* yes," she groaned. "I'm going to come soon if you keep doing that. I'm getting close–"

While I watched her gaping mouth and the flush on her cheeks beginning to spread down over her neck onto the top of her chest, I couldn't resist touching her in more intimate areas, and as she began to tilt her head back, I snaked my right hand around the side of her ass, inserting two fingers into her sopping hole.

"Oh my God, Jade," Piper grunted. "That feels so good! Finger my pussy while I fuck your beautiful body. I'm going to come so hard–"

"Yes, baby," I purred, gazing up into her contorting face. "Let it go. Spray your juices all over my pussy. Let me feel you cum all over me."

"Huff, huff, huff," Piper gasped, approaching the turning point. Suddenly, she exhaled with a deep animal sound while mashing her vulva hard against the top of my pubic bone as she began jetting her juices all over my hand pressed hard against her contracting pussy.

"Ngah!" she hissed, peering into my eyes as her head jerked in spastic convulsions in tandem with the contractions she was feeling further below.

I pulled her head down toward mine and kissed her hard on the lips while she grunted into my mouth, jerking my hips hard against hers as we listened to the sound of other couples around the room reaching their own climaxes in blissful harmony. When the room finally fell silent and Piper collapsed onto the mat beside me, we peered around the room at the happy smiles on the faces of the other women who were panting and caressing one another softly.

"So, what did you all think?" Laila said, panning around the circle with a sly grin on her face. "Do you guys *still* think the missionary position is boring?"

"*Hell* no," Hailey panted, pinching her partner's nipples softly between her fingers.

"I'm glad you enjoyed it," Laila said, passing out some thick bath towels around the circle. "You might want to take a little rest while you take a few minutes to clean up. Because the *next* demonstration is going to ramp up the excitement to a whole other level."

While Piper and I began to mop up the puddle she'd left in the center of our mat, I smiled to myself thinking about how cleverly Laila had scheduled our workshops. As I peered at her juices dripping down the inside of both our thighs, I was happy to have paired up with one of the girls who'd attended the previous workshop where we'd learned to ejaculate stimulating our female prostate glands.

Laila wasn't kidding when she said a little waterworks will only add to the excitement, I smiled.

3

———

After everybody recovered from their orgasms, Laila asked for a new volunteer to demonstrate the next position. This time Trinity was the first to respond, and as she crawled over to kneel beside the workshop leader, Laila nodded at her with a smile.

"It's interesting that you chose to position yourself that way," she said. "Because in this next maneuver, there's going to be a lot of *kneeling*. I call it the *Praying Mantis*, not only because of the posture we'll be assuming, but also because in this case the one on top will be in a perfect position to gobble up the one on the bottom."

"Mmm," Trinity smiled. "It sounds delicious. Which one of us will be doing the gobbling?"

"As you're about to see, in this position we'll *both* get equal stimulation to the important parts, but it will be easier for me to demonstrate the many variations with me on top. So, if you'd like to lie down with your legs slightly parted, we can begin."

"It sounds similar to the start of the missionary position..."

"It might seem that way, but I assure you this will be a very different experience, one in which both partners can take an active role."

Laila crawled between Trinity's legs then she lifted one knee over the outside of her partner's hips while pressing the inside of her other thigh firmly against Trinity's pussy.

"Mmm, you're so *soft*," Trinity purred, rocking her hips gently against Laila's inner thigh.

"That's not the *only* soft part you'll feel in this position," Laila smiled, lying back on the mat as she pressed her left leg under Trinity's right thigh.

"In this variation of the classic scissoring position, we both have equal control over how we can stimulate our vulvas. It can be kind of fun when you feel like a slow, languorous fuck first thing in the morning."

Laila propped herself back up on her knees while tilting Trinity's body forty-five degrees toward her.

"But I find the *kneeling* position offers more opportunities to grind our pussies together while also providing a direct focal point to each other's upper bodies, where we can kiss and play with certain *other* erogenous areas..."

As Laila leaned forward, she began to gyrate her hips in a rotational movement over Trinity's angled pussy, creating some loud slurping noises. Those of us in a position to view what was going on behind them lowered our heads and gasped when we saw their two pussies gnashing together.

"Holy *fuck*," Trinity groaned. "I feel every inch of your pussy fucking me in this position. I'm kind of glad I'm on the *bottom* this time."

"It can be even *more* fun being the one on top," Laila said, grabbing Trinity's right knee and pulling it toward her chest. "You've got more leverage this way, and you can really dial up the action once you get properly warmed up."

"I'm definitely beginning to get warmed up," Trinity panted. "It feels incredible having your pussy touching me like that."

Laila smiled, tilting her hips forward a few degrees while Trinity uttered a deep, guttural moan.

"And in this position, we can also rub our *clits* together as hard as we want also."

"That is so hot," one of the girls behind the tribbing couple groaned, pressing two fingers into her pussy while she gaped at Laila's and Trinity's labia stretching and pulling while they rubbed their vulvas together.

"It can be quite a feast if you have a *third* partner in the mix," Laila nodded. "She can lie with her head at the junction of your two hips while she licks *both* of your vulvas."

"Were you looking for another volunteer?" I said, raising my hand.

"Maybe on our last day," Laila chuckled, pulling Trinity's foot higher in the air until her leg was pointing straight up, pinned tightly between Laila's plump breasts.

"Feel free to experiment with your partner's body in this position," she continued. "If she's *especially* flexible, you can really open up her undercarriage for a more direct attack."

While Laila gently pressed her upper body forward, Trinity's extended leg moved closer toward her chest, until Laila was leaning directly down over her abdomen with Trinity's foot pressed all the way beside her head.

"You're pretty flexible," Laila nodded, kissing Trinity softly on the lips while she rolled her pussy over her stretched gash.

"Holy fuck–" Piper muttered next to me, mesmerized by the sight of the two women locked in a wide-open scissor position with both of their dripping pussies clearly exposed.

"It's pretty hot, I have to admit," Laila said, lifting herself up while pulling back Trinity's pinned leg as she crawled off her partner and rested on the duvet in her customary cross-legged position.

"Oh my God," Trinity panted, placing her hands behind her back as she rubbed her slippery thighs together. "I haven't been fucked like that since my girlfriend tied me to my bedposts. Somebody better jump on me soon, or I'm going to burst a gasket."

"I'm pretty sure you won't have much trouble finding willing partners from the look of it," Laila chuckled, noticing half the women around the circle still moving their hands between their legs. "But in the interest of sharing the spoils, this time I'd like one person from each mat to move clockwise to the next position in the circle. That way, by the time we end our workshop, everyone will have had a chance to partner up with every other person in the group."

I peered around the circle, counting the yoga mats distributed like hour markers on a clock.

"If I'm doing my math right," I said. "That means we can look forward to ten more tribbing exercises before we finish the workshop?"

"I suspect it will be even *more* by the time we introduce some toys and multiple partners into the mix," Laila smiled. "But I wouldn't worry about keeping track at this point. There should be more than enough notches on your bedpost by the time we finish up here. So go ahead and shift one position to your left and give this new position a try. If you liked the missionary position, I have a feeling you're going to find this one takes your tribbing experience to a whole new level."

Piper suddenly turned to look at me with a wrinkled brow.

"Would you like to switch positions, or should I?" she said.

I peered over her shoulder noticing Hailey crawling toward our mat like a stalking cat.

"I feel pretty damn hungry about now," she growled. "Which of you two girls feels like getting gobbled up?"

"I have a feeling Piper might like being on the *bottom* this time," I smiled. "Why don't you guys enjoy yourself this time and I'll circle back a little later?"

"I'll look forward to that," Hailey grinned, grabbing Piper's hand and pulling her toward her, kissing her hard on her lips.

As the two women reclined onto the mat with Hailey in the superior position, I shuffled over to the next mat and smiled at a pretty brunette about my age.

"I'm Ashley," she said, holding out her hand awkwardly.

"Jade," I said, clasping her sweaty palm softly. "No need for us to be so formal, with us about to get all twisted up in knots in a few minutes."

"No, I suppose not," she chuckled, sitting back on her heels as she appraised my naked body positioned directly in front of her. "How should we decide who goes on top this time?"

"From the looks of it," I said, tilting my head toward the middle of the circle where Laila had just completed her demonstration. "I don't think it matters. But just to be fair, why don't we do rock, paper, scissors?"

"Aha," Ashley laughed. "Very clever. Winner goes on top?"

"Deal," I nodded.

We each held out our fists, then we pumped them together three times, straightening our palms on the last pump. I chose paper and Ashley displayed scissors, so that meant I'd be taking the superior position this time.

"I'm not really sure there'll be a loser in this instance," I smiled. "But I guess *one* of us has to play the role of the mantis while the other one pretends to be her prey."

"I'm ready to get gobbled up," Ashley nodded, lying down on the mat with her legs spread wide apart. "Feast away."

"Mmm," I hummed, peering down at her glistening pink labia. "Don't mind if I do."

I shimmied my body up between her thighs and lifted one knee over her hip while positioning my other one against her dripping pussy.

"So you prefer the *kneeling* position over the traditional posture?" Ashley said, gazing up at me.

"Laila named it the Praying Mantis for a reason," I grinned, glancing at her tits rolling softly to her side. "I plan on taking maximum advantage while you're pinned underneath me. There's a few tasty morsels I'd like to sample before I go in for the main course."

"As long as you don't bite my *head* off before you're finished," Ashley chuckled.

I leaned forward and pressed my lips against her face, biting her lip gently.

"Not right away," I smiled, pulling away temporarily. "At least not until I feast on your *other* your succulent parts."

"Yes," Ashley grunted, feeling my pussy pressing against hers as she tilted her hips to join our vulvas together. "Impale me with that weapon of yours. Split me open like a ripe melon."

"Fucking right," I growled, grabbing her thigh and pulling it hard against my stomach as I began to gnash my pussy against hers.

I could feel her puffy labia rolling over mine as I tribbed her slit with our gashes sliding over one another, intertwining like a sexy pussy kiss.

"Holy shit," Ashley panted. "You feel so *hot*!"

"And you feel so *juicy*," I groaned.

"Oh yeah?" Ashley grinned, staring up at me. "Do you think I've got enough to whet your appetite?"

"Fuck yes," I hissed. "I only wish I was wearing a *dildo*, so I could sink my cock deep inside those thick folds or yours. You feel absolutely delicious."

"Pull up a little higher," Ashley panted, reaching out to pinch my nipples. "I want to feel you rubbing on something a little harder..."

Understanding exactly what she meant, I tilted my hips forward a few more inches and placed my hand under her ass, pressing her pubic bone harder against mine. I felt our hard nubs touching together, and I mashed my pussy harder against her.

"*Yes*, Jade," Ashley grunted. "Right there. Fuck my pussy right there. Make me come all over your hot snatch."

Watching her face peering up at me with unbridled ecstasy was too much for me to resist, and as I lowered my face onto hers, I pulled her knee toward her chest, kissing her passionately while we ground our cunts together. There was something incredibly sexy about the lips of her mouth sliding in and out of mine while our lower lips gnashed and dripped over one another at the same time. As we both began to grunt louder into each other's mouths while grabbing each other's buttocks, I glanced over at the mat next to me watching Hailey hammering her hips between Piper's legs while she pulled one of the redhead's legs hard up against her chest.

"*Oh fuck, oh fuck...*" Ashley huffed underneath me. "I'm

going to come, Jade. I'm going to come so hard all over your beautiful, wet pussy."

"Yes, baby," I grunted. "Gush all over me. I'm ready to take my prize."

"Ieeee!" Ashley squealed with one final powerful exhalation as her hips began quaking while she screamed into my mouth.

When I felt her jerking against our connected pussies, I couldn't hold back any longer and all the pent-up pleasure I'd been holding back suddenly exploded while I gushed all over her stretched slit like a dormant geyser. I must have squirted a gallon of juices over her upturned ass by the time I finished squirting in powerful contractions. When we both finished convulsing in each other's arms, I held her with her leg still pressed tightly over my chest, savoring the feeling of our sopping pussies pulsing and dribbling over one another.

"Where the hell did you learn to do *that*?" Ashley said when I finally pulled away.

"You mean that squirting thing?" I smiled.

"It felt more like a *waterfall*," she panted, still trying to catch her breath.

"I've been doing that for a while now, but Laila taught some of us how to really turn on the faucets at her female ejaculation workshop."

"I've got to learn that trick on my *own* some day," she said. "If you were a *real* praying mantis, I'm pretty sure you would have basted and sauteed me more than enough to finish the rest of your meal."

"Don't *tempt* me," I said, glancing down at her dripping folds. "If we weren't restricted to touching only our pussies together, I wouldn't hesitate to lap up the *rest* of you for dessert right now."

4

———————

I t didn't take long after Ashley, Piper, Hailey and I came for the rest of the girls in the room to reach their own climaxes. It was quite a sight watching all the other couples scissoring their figures together in a ring of twisted, shaking bodies. After everyone had a chance to recover and clean up, we took a break to enjoy a catered lunch of lobster rolls, potato salad, and Pellegrino. While we sat around the circle in our terrycloth robes, each of us couldn't help peering beside us to see who we'd be paired up with next.

On the mat to my left sat Trinity and a cute blonde girl who looked barely out of high school. As they nibbled on their food, they glanced in both directions, trying to guess which person from each pair would move to the next position. With four different potential combinations at each turn, the experience felt a bit like an erotic game of musical chairs.

I peered over at Laila who was making small talk with one of the couples sitting next to her and smiled at her ingenuity conceiving of another workshop that was equal parts stimulating and educational. I wondered how many of the participants had signed up to discover new techniques to spice up their love lives versus just looking for an chance to stare at a bunch of naked women having sex. Either way, I suspected her seminar had already exceeded many of their expectations, and I was looking forward to what she had planned for the rest of our session.

When everybody finished eating, we all sat back on our mats in the same cross-legged position as Laila, facing her expectantly. I couldn't help but giggle at how quickly she'd gotten all of us under her thumb, not to mention her sexy, naked hips.

"I hope everyone had a chance to rehydrate and recharge your batteries," she smiled. "Because this afternoon we're going to ramp up the action with three new exercises that will stretch your resources to the limit."

Exercises, I chuckled to myself. *That's one name for them.* Something told me I'd be feeling the after-effects of this workshop in more places than one by the time we finished.

"Are you guys ready to learn some more exciting new techniques?" she said.

Everybody nodded excitedly while she peered around the circle looking for a new candidate to demonstrate the next position.

"Any volunteers for our next demonstration?"

Everyone's hand flew up instantly, and Laila paused, glancing at the mat next to mine.

"*Becky*, isn't it?" she said, staring straight into the eyes of the cute coed sitting beside me.

The blonde girl smiled and Laila curled her finger in a come-hither motion toward her mat, inviting her to come to the center of the circle.

"We're going to test those quick reflexes of yours with

this next position," Laila smiled, patting the futon beside her. "I call this one the *Reverse Cowgirl*, partly because one of us will be riding the other like a horse, but *also* because she'll will be faced in the opposite direction."

"Does that mean we won't be able to look at each other while we're doing it?" Becky said with wide eyes.

"Oh, we'll be able to *look* at each other alright," Laila grinned. "Just not at each other's faces. But I suspect we'll be able to find certain *other* body parts to keep ourselves entertained."

"Which of us will be the rider?" Becky asked innocently. "And who'll be playing the role of the horse?"

"Since you put it that way," Laila chuckled. "Why don't *you* be the one on top this time? It's a fairly simple procedure, and I can guide you just as easily from the bottom. But you might want to find something to hold onto. I can't account for how much *bucking* I might do once we get into the action."

Laila pulled off her robe, then lay face up on the futon with her legs extended straight out in front of her.

"How would you like me to position myself?" Becky said.

"This one's pretty straight-forward," Laila nodded. "You simply sit overtop of me facing my feet with your knees straddling my hips."

"Okay," Becky said, pulling off her robe and angling one of her legs awkwardly over Laila's naked midsection.

"Not so much on my *stomach* as my hips," Laila grunted, trying to catch her breath. "Unless you also want to *suffocate* me while you're fucking me."

"That wouldn't be much fun," the girl said, sliding her hips forward over Laila's lower abdomen, leaving a glistening streak down the middle of her stomach. "I don't think the rest of the group would like that very much."

While gentle laughter spread around the circle, Laila placed her hands on opposite sides of Becky's ass, pushing her forward a few more inches.

"In this position," she continued, "the trick is to tilt your hips at just the right angle and position your hips in precisely the right spot over my mound to get the best friction with your clitoris."

"Yes..." Becky grunted, rocking her hips softly over Laila's pelvis. "I think I found the spot."

"Now it's just a matter of you riding me to your heart's content," Laila smiled. "While trying not to fall off as your pleasure continues to rise."

"What about *you*?" Becky said, rocking her hips back and forth over Laila's hard pubis, leaving a wet slick on her lower abdomen.

"This position is mostly intended for the enjoyment of the one on *top*, but if you tilt your body forward a little further and shift a few inches lower down, you might be able to feel something a little *softer* for you to rub against."

Becky placed her hands on the floor beside Laila's knees, then she leaned forward about forty-five degrees, angling her ass up toward Laila's face. I smiled, beginning to realize that Laila hadn't chosen to be on the bottom by accident, having a perfect bird's-eye view of Becky's tight ass and exposed pucker.

"Yes," Laila panted, raising her head to stare at Becky's gyrating hips. "Do you feel anything different in this angle?"

"I feel your pussy rubbing against mine now," she nodded. "I like this position better. You're softer, and *wetter*."

"Mmm," Laila grunted. "I'm not sure which of us is getting wetter faster. I can already feel your juices running down over my labia."

The girls at the end of the circle lowered their heads to

stare at the two women mashing their slits together while the women on the opposite end tilted their faces to peer at Becky's exposed rosebud stretching and puckering while she flexed her buttock muscles.

Unfortunately, in my position directly beside the tribbing couple, Becky's thigh was obscuring my view of their most interesting parts. But that didn't stop me from staring at her pretty tits shaking on her chest as she pistoned her hips over Laila's slit, approaching the peak of her pleasure.

"Okay," Laila said, grabbing the sides of Becky's ass, sitting up against her heaving back. "I wouldn't want you to drain *all* your energy before your partner gets to participate in this little rodeo ride. Why don't you go back to your mat to finish the demonstration? As before, I'd like one of you to move one position to your left to find a new partner. You might have to arm wrestle to determine who goes on top, but either way, I'm pretty sure you'll *both* enjoy the experience."

While Becky returned to her mat beside Trinity, Ashley and I peered at one another with lopsided grins.

"Rock, paper, scissors?" she said, unsure which of us should move to the next mat.

I looked behind her, noticing a full-figured girl looking like a dead-ringer of the pretty actress Christina Hendricks shuffling toward us.

"I have a feeling you're going to enjoy riding this next horse," I nodded, glancing behind me toward Becky's mat. "I'm gonna see if I can take a turn with that pretty co-ed."

"It shouldn't take long from the looks of it," Ashley said, peering down at Becky's dripping thighs.

"Catch you later, alligator," I smiled, crawling over to Becky's mat.

"In a while, crocodile," she nodded.

As excited as I was to mix it up with the pretty African-American girl, I was happy when Trinity chose to move to the next mat, leaving Becky all for myself.

"Hi," I said, stretching out my hand. "I'm Jade."

"I guess you know *my* name by now," Becky chuckled, clasping my hand with her slippery fingers. "Did you have a preference for how you'd like to play this one?"

"Something tells me *you're* in more of a hurry to finish this ride than me," I smiled, pinching her erect nipples softly between my fingers. "I have a feeling I'm going to enjoy watching you more from the *bottom* than with me on top."

"I was hoping you'd say that," she said, climbing on top of me as I lay down on the yoga mat. "Do you want me sitting up or leaning slightly forward?"

"Whichever way gives you the best stimulation," I smiled, caressing the sides of her ass.

"Mmm," she purred, rocking her wet pussy over my hard mound. "I'm already halfway there. This shouldn't take long, then I can focus on giving you some more attention."

"Let it rip baby," I said, squeezing her buttock muscles as she ground her cunt against my pubis. "Don't worry about me."

"Oh God," she panted. "That feels so good–"

"It *looks* pretty damn fine too," I groaned, watching her chest rising and falling as she began to breathe more rapidly.

"Oh fuck, Jade," she hissed. "I'm going to come. I can't hold it back any longer...."

She dropped her hands on top of my thighs looking for support, and I dug my fingernails into the side of her hips while her buttock muscles started quivering as she shuddered and groaned atop my hips. There was something incredibly sexy about not being able to see her face as I listened to her orgasm and watch the muscles in her back and buttocks twitching while she spread her knees wider over my hips.

Even though I'd barely had any time to begin getting worked up myself, I somehow found the experience even more gratifying than if I'd come myself. Fortunately, it didn't take long for her to resume her gentle rocking over my hips, and as she slid her vulva over the crest of my symphysis, she turned her head partly in my direction, revealing her flushed face.

"Would you like me to try this in a *different* position?" she said. "I'm ready for some more action if you are."

"Oh, I'm definitely *ready*," I growled, slapping the sides of her ass with both hands. "Ride me like a bucking bronco. You fit perfectly into my saddle."

"Mmm," Becky groaned, tilting her upper body lower as her cheeks began to spread apart, revealing her pink sphincter. "I think I can feel the *horn* of your saddle."

"Yes, baby," I groaned, feeling her nub sliding over mine as our slits meshed together. "Rub your clit against mine while I feel your juices dripping down my pussy. You're so warm and wet..."

"Not as wet as *you*," Becky said, tilting her head down to peer between her legs at my glistening slit. "Spread your legs a little further apart so I can see your juicy pussy. This is so fucking hot watching you this way."

Her dirty talk caught me be surprise, and I quickly spread my legs, pressing her knees further out to the side as her ass tilted higher toward my face.

"I've got a hell of a view watching *you* from this angle too," I moaned, feeling her wet vulva sliding over mine.

"Do you like watching my ass while I ride you from behind?" she said.

"Damn *straight*," I grunted, digging my nails harder into the back of her buttocks while I watched her pucker flexing as she ground her pussy over the top of my pubis.

"I'm going to come again," she huffed, gripping the top of my thighs tightly with her hands. "I hope you don't mind. This is just too damn hot..."

"I'm going to come too," I groaned, feeling my orgasm approaching like a freight train. "Keep grinding my clit just like that–"

"Oh *fuck*!" Becky rasped, pressing her chest down onto the mat between my legs while she humped my slit with her mound.

Suddenly, her rosebud began clamping in rhythmic contractions as she panted in muffled moans onto the mat. The sight of her pretty pucker flexing in powerful contractions while her buttock muscles quivered inches away from my face was too much for me to resist, and within seconds I felt the build-up of juices inside my pussy beginning to jet out in strong spurts all over her pussy and lower abdomen.

"What the hell...?" I Becky panted as I squirted all over our joined pussies while we shuddered in mutual pleasure.

I'd been so preoccupied staring at her pretty ass and focusing on our *own* pleasure that I hardly even noticed when the rest of the girls around the circle erupted in a cacophony of simultaneous pleasure, twisting and shaking their bodies together in the same position.

Holy shit, I thought to myself. *Just when I thought I'd seen and tried everything. Laila wasn't kidding when she said we'd learn a few new tricks when I signed up for her latest workshop.*

5

———————

While we all lay in a tangled heap on our mats panting and heaving from our powerful orgasms, Laila peered around the circle and smiled.

"It looks like everyone found a way to get something out of that exercise," she grinned. "If you liked a little ass humping, I think you'll find our next position will *double* your pleasure. Who'd like to be my next volunteer?"

Once again, everybody's hand quickly flew up, and Laila paused while she contemplated who to choose. After a few seconds, she turned toward Ashley and her partner still squirming excitedly on their mat.

"How about it, Paige?" she said, peering at the full-figured redhead. "Have you recovered sufficiently from your last engagement to give it another try?"

"I'm *always* ready for some more girl-on-girl action," she smiled, crawling seductively on all fours toward the center of the ring.

As she slunk toward Laila, every pair of eyes in the room stared at her magnificent ass, shining under the overhead lights like a Rubenesque masterpiece. Even though she was more full-figured than the other women attending the workshop, there wasn't a trace of cellulite on her backside, and I could hear myself panting while I watched her slit winking at me as she parted her thighs. When she reached Laila's position, she sat down next to her while everybody feasted their eyes over her equally well-endowed, plump round tits.

"In this *next* position," Laila said, not skipping a beat, "we'll *both* be faced in opposite directions. "I like to call it *Ass Backwards*, because we'll be rubbing our butts while facing away from each other."

Laila peered at Paige, lifting an eyebrow.

"Are you ready to give it a whirl?" she said to the pretty redhead.

"Absolutely," Paige said, rising up onto her knees. "How would you like me to position myself?"

"This one starts out pretty straight-forward," Laila said, moving into a doggy position beside Paige. "But there's a few interesting variations we can try to mix it up. Let's start by getting on all fours facing away from each other, then touch our asses together–"

"Only our *asses*?" Paige said, copying the workshop leader's posture and shuffling backwards until her stout derriere pressed against Laila's.

"We'll have to work at maneuvering our bodies a little to create some friction in the interesting places," Laila nodded. "But that's half the fun."

As she began to roll her hips over the back of Paige's ass, I noticed a sheen of shiny fluid on the redhead's skin.

"Sometimes it helps to spread some *lube* over your asses to heighten the experience," Laila said, pressing her ass into the soft creases and folds of Paige's fleshy backside. "Since you won't be touching your *pussies* right away, you might need a little extra lubrication to get started."

Paige smiled, glancing toward her previous partner, Ashley.

"I think I've still got plenty of natural lube covering my ass from my *last* exercise," she nodded.

"So it would seem," Laila purred, enjoying the feeling of Paige's plump rump massaging her backside.

"This is a sexy way for two women to warm up with a little foreplay," she said. "But if you tilt your upper bodies toward the floor, this will bring a *different* part of your anatomy together..."

As Laila lowered her shoulders, her hips temporarily pulled away from Paige's, and I noticed her slit flaring open with her clit poking out from the top of her folds. Both women spread their knees wider apart and when they reconnected their asses, they both groaned.

"*Fuck*, that feels hot," Paige grunted, rocking her hips up and down as she slid her pussy over Laila's. "I can feel every inch of your skin sliding against me."

"It's a great way to grind your pussies together while facing away from each other," Laila nodded. "It can be even *more* exciting using a double-sided dildo, which we'll introduce at our session tomorrow. But don't discount how much fun it can be to just grind your asses together. Your backside is more sensitive than you might imagine."

"Oh, I can *imagine*," Hailey moaned from the other side of the circle while she rolled her fingers over her wet pussy, gawking at Paige's beautiful ass.

"There's a reason why gay men like to fuck each other up the ass," Laila said, pressing her buttocks harder against Paige's soft butt, beginning to spread her cheeks apart. "The anal sphincter is surrounded with many sensitive nerve endings and can be very pleasant to stimulate in its own way, as some of you may have discovered while performing oral sex with your partners."

"Nnghh," Paige suddenly groaned, feeling Laila's rosebud sliding over her own. "It feels even better with your *pussy* stimulating me there."

"If you *really* want to dive in and go to town," Laila said, raising her left knee and placing it on the outside of Paige's opposite knee resting on the floor. "You can angle your bodies into an inverted *scissor* position while you rub your asses together. This allows you to slide your leg into your partner's *crack*, stimulating both her pussy and her anus while you're grinding your hips together.

"Oh my God," Paige grunted, grabbing Laila's inside knee and pulling it harder against her stomach. "I'm going to *come* if you keep doing that. I can feel you rubbing me all the way down my perineum."

"Exactly," Laila said, humping Paige's ass harder for a few seconds before pulling her leg out from under her belly and turning around to kneel behind her in a doggy-style position. "And when you want to mix it up a bit further, you can always shift position to give your partner a proper ass fucking, which of course is even more exciting when you're wearing a strap-on."

Laila dry-humped Paige's ass for a few moments, then she pushed her forward, collapsing her body onto the futon.

"But *sometimes*," she said with a glint in her eye. "I just like to fuck my partner's ass with my pussy while she's pinned underneath me. There's nothing hotter than cumming all over your partner's body when there's nothing she can do about it."

No wonder she chose Paige for this demonstration, I smiled. *I'd fuck that ass any chance I had an opportunity also.*

"No fair!" Paige grunted while pinned under Laila's spread-eagled thighs. "I was just about to *come*. You're such a tease!"

"That's half the fun with this position," Laila said, lifting her leg and flopping back onto the futon beside Paige with her knees crossed.

"Screw *that*," Paige said, raising herself off the futon and peering into Laila's eyes with flushed cheeks. "Are you *ever* going to let your partner come during one of these demonstrations? Because this whole setup seems a little lopsided in your favor..."

"That's why I'm the one in charge," Laila smiled. "I get to call the shots while you enjoy the spoils. But never fear, you shouldn't have any trouble finding some other willing partners for you to finish your demonstration. I just wanted to get you warmed up..."

I looked at Laila, twirling my finger in the air to signal that each of us should move to the next position in the circle.

"Same as before?" I said.

"Yes," Laila nodded. "We're only halfway done completing the circle. It's almost as much fun trying out each new position as it is with a different partner. One person from each mat should move clockwise to the left."

Becky and I glanced at one another, and when I saw Paige crawling toward our mat, I smiled, excited to give the two redheads a chance to pair up.

"Why don't you stay here and help Paige finish her exercise?" I said, noticing Trinity hanging behind on the next mat, waiting for me to move over. "Maybe we'll have a chance to connect a little later in the workshop."

"I hope so," Becky said, peering wide-eyed at Paige crawling toward her like a lion approaching its prey.

When I shuffled over to the next mat, Trinity kissed me with a familiar embrace.

"I was *wondering* when I'd get another turn with you," she said, remembering out last hookup at Laila's Circle Jill workshop. "I wasn't sure you'd be able to resist fucking that gorgeous redhead after watching her shake her booty in the ring with Laila."

"It crossed my mind," I smiled. "But I think I'll enjoy *watching* her have her way with the pretty coed as much as having her for myself. Besides, I've waited too long to take a piece of *another* pretty ass..."

As the two of us began kissing, I glanced over at Becky and Paige who were already rubbing their asses together while Becky struggled to stay upright as Paige slapped her thick derriere against her backside.

"Are you just gonna sit there and *watch*?" Trinity said, sliding her hand around the back of my ass while she kissed me, pressing her fingers into my crease. "Or do you want to sample some of this for yourself?"

"You're twisting my arm," I said, turning around and lifting my ass in the air while positioning myself in the doggy position.

Trinity got down on all fours and pressed her butt up against mine, and within seconds we were twisting our asses together, groaning in pleasure as our wet pussies slid over one another. Impatient to feel her clit against mine, I tilted my upper body down toward the floor, staring at her tits swaying back and forth as she tribbed me from behind. Eager to do the same, she leaned down, and we smiled at each other while we slapped our asses together.

Finding it difficult to gain traction on our clits, she lifted one knee and straddled my leg on the floor while pressing her right thigh under my belly. With the underside of her leg now resting against my mound and her warm skin rubbing along the full length of my perineum, I pressed my own thigh hard against her pussy.

We grabbed each other's legs and began to slide our cracks together, and as I felt her rosebud rub over mine, we both moaned. It didn't take long for the two of us to begin squirming in delight as we both moved closer and closer toward orgasm. I couldn't see her face with our asses blocking the view diagonally toward one another in this upside-down scissor position, but the feeling of our slippery pussies and asses rubbing together was more than enough to take me to the edge.

"I'm almost there," I panted, pulling her thigh harder against my pussy. "Are you getting close?"

"Yes," she said. "Do you think you can squirt again like we learned at the last workshop?"

"Fuck, yes," I groaned. "I feel like I'm going to burst a gasket any moment now..."

"Let it rip, baby," Trinity grunted. "I'm going to come with you. Let's see who can squirt harder–"

Suddenly she squealed like a cat, shaking her hips rapidly against my ass while she sprayed her juices all over the yoga mat and our exposed bellies. When I felt her cumming against my pussy, I started squirting along with her, spraying our combined juices in every direction between our splayed legs. By the time we finished shaking and spurting, we collapsed onto the mat laughing like a pair of schoolgirls while we rolled in the warm puddle underneath us.

Moments later, we heard loud grunting coming from the mat next to us, and we peered over watching Paige arching over Becky's pinned ass while she fucked the coed roughly from behind. While the girl held onto the edge of their yoga mat tightly with two hands to keep from sliding off, Paige pressed her hands onto the floor beside her chest as her thick buttock muscles flexed powerfully, approaching another climax.

When she finally came, she pressed her pussy hard against Becky's smaller ass, shaking her globes violently while she squirted one hard jet after another down Becky's crack and over her dripping pussy. As the two of us gazed at them in amazement, the rest of the room suddenly became silent while everybody else watched in rapt attention.

"Looks like we aren't the *only* ones who learned how to squirt at one of Laila's workshops," Trinity grinned, caressing my breasts softly while we lay beside one another watching the couple.

"Yeah," I said. "I just hope Becky will still be able to *walk* after that pounding. I'm not sure her body will be able to take much more of this exercise..."

6

After Paige rolled over Becky and collapsed onto their mat, I glanced up at the clock in Laila's living room, surprised at how late it was in the day. We'd all been so captivated learning and practicing her exciting tribbing techniques, that we'd completely lost track of time.

"I'm glad everyone seemed to enjoy that last position," Laila smiled. "I think we might have time left for one more demonstration. Who's up for one last exercise?"

Everyone raised their hands again and as Laila teasingly peered around the circle, she abruptly stopped, staring straight at me.

"What do you say, Jade?" she grinned. "Are you ready for another sexy demonstration for the full group?"

I wasn't sure if she was referring to our *current* session or the last workshop where we'd finished with the two of us connected with a double-ended dildo while we squirted all over each other's pussies.

"I thought you'd never ask," I smiled, slinking toward her.

"This next position might be the sexiest one yet," Laila said, peering at me with a sly grin. "I like to call it *Hip-Hop* because of the way we'll be grinding our hips together. But we won't just be rubbing our pussies together. In this position, we'll be rubbing *everything* together."

"Mmm," I purred, feeling my juices dribbling out of my slit again. "It sounds delicious. Who gets to be on top this time?"

Laila paused, peering up at the clock.

"I'm not sure I can trust you to stop before we run out of time," she said.

"I didn't realize we were on a *limit*," I said. "I thought you said at our last workshop that when it comes to two women making love, our focus should be on the *journey* rather than the destination?"

"That's true," she smiled, swiping the back of her hand gently over my breast. "But we still have two days left in this workshop. We've got to leave a *few* surprises for the rest of the group."

"Yes," I grinned, leaning in to kiss her on the lips. "And I know from previous experience how full of *surprises* you can be."

"You have no idea," she said, pushing me softly down onto the futon. "Lie back with your knees angled up toward your chest. We're going to give the girls a memorable experience to keep them motivated for tomorrow."

I did as Laila instructed, and as my slit began to stretch apart from my retracted legs, I reflected back at our last encounter at her Fountain of Venus workshop. Feeling exposed with my hole staring her straight in the face, I half hoped she'd pull out another one of her special dildos to fuck me hard in front of the group. But instead, she stood up straddling my waist with two legs, then she slowly squatted down until the bottom of her thighs rested overtop of mine. When our pussies touched, I groaned and reached out to squeeze her tits dangling inches from my face. She leaned forward, and our lips met while we moaned in each other's mouths.

"I've been looking forward to *this* one all day," she whispered next to my ear as she began to grind her hips against mine.

With the sound of our wet pussies rolling over one another beginning to spread around the room, I glanced out of the corner of my eye, noticing the girls on the opposite side of the circle leaning down to gawk at our exposed pussies mashing together on our upturned asses.

"I I when I'd have another chance to connect with you," I moaned, peering into her eyes. "Ever since you sent me your latest invitation to this new workshop, it's all I've been able to think about."

"Oh?" Laila grunted overtop of me. "Have you been practicing alone while thinking about me?"

"Fuck, yes," I said, pulling her harder toward me, feeling her sweaty breasts pressing up against mine. "You have no idea how many times I've squirted imagining it was I fucking me instead of one of my vibrators."

"Well, I'm fucking you *now*," she moaned, slapping her hips up and down over mine. "Though I *do* have plans for introducing some toys later in the workshop."

As Laila lifted her pussy away from mine, I felt her dribbling overtop of me while a band of lubrication stretched between our two slits.

"Oh my Gawd..." someone muttered from the other end of the circle, and I turned my head to see half the women fingering themselves while they watched our slapping pussies.

"I see you've made some progress learning to relax your prostate," Laila whispered into my ear, referring to the special gland next to our G-spot that held the reservoir of lubricating fluid designed to facilitate reproduction.

"I never was one to let a little wetness get in the way of having fun," I smiled. "But I like to save the best for last."

"Do you think you can *come* for me in this position?" Laila grunted into my ear. "We could give the girls a hell of a show with our asses turned up together this way."

I pulled back a few inches, peering at her with a surprised expression.

"Were you thinking of breaking your rule about saving our orgasms for our own partners?" I smiled.

"I'm considering it," she panted, peering up at the clock. "We don't have enough time to finish up with the *rest* of the group anyway. Let's give them something to *fantasize* about until tomorrow."

"You don't have to ask me twice," I groaned, pulling Laila's face harder down onto mine, fucking her mouth with my tongue.

As she slapped her butt over mine, we ground our pussies harder together feeling our juices pouring out of our holes and down the crack of my ass. Just when I thought it couldn't get any better, Laila suddenly raised her hips six inches over mine and started squirting hard all over my exposed slit and anus. The jetting stimulation on my clit only added to my already heightened sense of arousal, and the combined sensation of her rubbing ass and her squirting pussy quickly took me over the edge as I rocked my body along with her while my anus clamped open and shut in powerful contractions. As we both jetted powerful squirts against our flapping pussies, the rest of the group groaned in simultaneous delight, coming along with us while we held onto each other tightly.

Fuck me, I smiled as we held each other like two mating toads on a lily pad. *I have no idea what she has in store for the next two days of our workshop, but if it's going to be anything like this, I better drink plenty of water to replenish my fluids.*

Because something tells me there's going to be a whole different kind of Fountain of Venus erupting tomorrow.

R eady for some even hotter exercises in Laila's latest all-girl scissoring workshop? Preorder the next exciting instalment in the lesbian mini-series, *Tribadism 2*, to see what happens next:

Just when you thought two women rubbing their bodies together couldn't get any sexier...

ALSO BY VICTORIA RUSH

Wet your whistle a hundred different ways with Jade's Erotic Adventures. Browse the full collection of Victoria Rush steamy stories here:

Click to scan your favorites...

FOLLOW VICTORIA RUSH:

Want to keep informed of my latest erotic book releases? Sign up for my newsletter and receive a FREE bonus book:

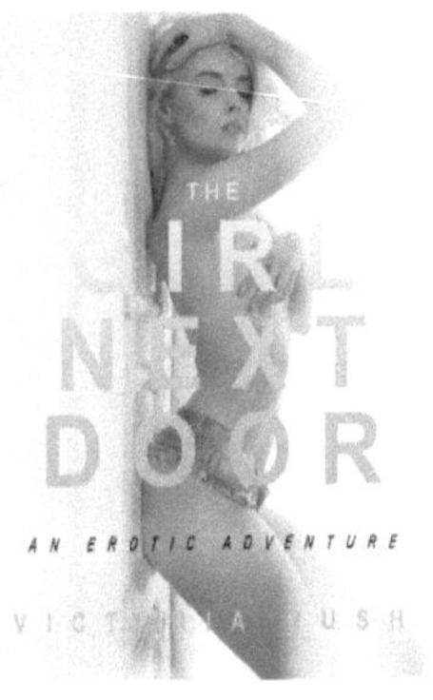

Spying on the neighbors just got a lot more interesting...